The Lima Bear ™ Stories

THE CAVE MONSTER

Story By Charles A. Neebe
Illustrations By Len DiSalvo

Lima Bear Press, LLC
PO Box 354
Montchanin, DE 19710-0354
Phone/fax: 302-691-4799
email: lbp.books@yahoo.com   website: www.limabearpress.com

Book design by: Len DiSalvo and George Clements
Cover design by: Len DiSalvo and George Clements
ISBN: 978-1-933872-32-2

Library of Congress Control Number: 2007931988

Printed in China
Published by Lima Bear Press
PO Box 354, Montchanin, DE 19710-0354
Bulk Orders: lbp.books@yahoo.com

The Lima Bear™ Stories

THE CAVE MONSTER

Story By Charles A. Neebe
Illustrations By Len DiSalvo

ACT 1

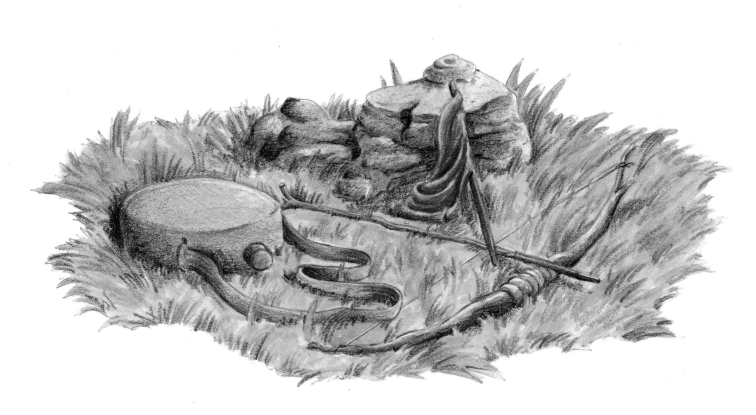

Lima Bear was swinging on his little swing waiting for his cousin, Sir L. Joe Bean, to arrive. Suddenly, Whistle-Toe the rabbit rushed up.

"Sir L. Joe Bean has been captured by the Cave Monster!" Whistle-Toe exclaimed.

"Oh, no! We must rescue him!" Lima Bear said.

Quickly, Lima Bear gathered two other friends - Maskamal the raccoon, and Back-Back the opossum. Now Back-Back was a very different kind of opossum. He had no back. Looking at him from behind, he was invisible - as if he had disappeared. That is how he got the name, Back-Back, in the first place.

"Where would the Cave Monster take him?" Whistle-Toe asked.

"Maybe some place where none of us has ever been," Lima Bear said. "Like Black Cave."

"Ba-ba-ba-lack Cave?" Maskamal said. "Wow-w-w-would we ever go there?"

"We have to," Lima Bear said bravely.

It was best to go at night in hopes that the Cave Monster would be asleep. Lima Bear said that each of them should think of something useful to bring. They met again before nightfall.

Whistle-Toe brought a canteen of water in case they got thirsty. Lima Bear brought two swords: his own sword and Sir L. Joe Bean's Royal Sword. The Royal Sword was special because it was gold with a diamond handle. But still, they did not look like swords. They looked more like small pins with tiny handles.

Maskamal brought a bow and arrow and red flag. The bow was made of a large stick bent over and tied with a piece of string. The arrow was a smaller stick. The arrow did not have any point at the end so Maskamal had painted the tip red instead. Back-Back could not think of anything useful to bring.

"That's all right," Maskamal said. "You hold the red flag."

"What for?" Back-Back asked.

"I have a plan," Maskamal said. "When we see the Cave Monster, you wave this red flag at him, and when he goes after you I will shoot him with my bow and arrow."

"Goes after me? I don't want him going after me. Here, you wave it, Maskamal. Let me shoot the arrow."

"You need to practice to shoot an arrow," Maskamal said. "Better you wave the flag."

"But what if you miss? What about me?"

"Don't worry. I'm a deadly shot. Here, I'll show you."

So Back-Back stood next to a tree and pretended it was the Cave Monster. While Back-Back waved the red flag at the tree, Maskamal, standing a few steps away, pulled the string of the bow as far as he could and took aim.

"Don't hit me, "Back-Back yelled.

"Fear not." The bow went 'twang' as Maskamal fired. The arrow fell out and landed in front of Maskamal's foot. They all stood there looking at the arrow on the ground.

"You are going to have to be awfully close to the Cave Monster to hit him with that bow and arrow," Lima Bear said.

"Isn't the Cave Monster going to have to be lying down on your feet?" Back-Back asked, now really scared.

"This arrow is no good," Maskamal said as he threw it away. "Let me try another one." He picked up a stick lying nearby.

"But the end of it isn't painted red," Lima Bear said.

"Oh, never mind," Maskamal said. He put it in his bow and aimed. "Start waving," he yelled to Back-Back. 'Twang'. The arrow flopped out of the bow. It just missed Maskamal's foot, landing right in front of him. "There, you see," he said. "A straight shot. A little more distance and it would have hit the tree dead center."

"I don't want to wave this flag at a real Cave Monster," Back-Back said.

"Don't worry," Maskamal said. "I just have to stand a little closer."

"I know," Lima Bear said. "Let's tie my sword to the end of your arrow. That will give it a sharp point." So with some tiny thread, they tied Lima Bear's little needle-sword onto the end.

Maskamal was very happy with his new arrow with a sharp point. "Now the Cave Monster had better watch out," he said.

But Back-Back still looked mighty worried.

Act 2

That night, the friends set out. Whistle-Toe led the way. Lima Bear was much too little to keep up, so he rode on Whistle-Toe's back, grabbing his fur to hold on.

At last they arrived. Ahead, they saw the dark entrance to Black Cave. The four friends stood in front of Black Cave. No one said anything. Each one was waiting for someone to do something.

"The Cave Monster is probably asleep," Whistle-Toe said.

"Maybe the Cave Monster doesn't sleep," Maskamal said.

"All monsters sleep," Whistle-Toe said. "Everyone knows that. Now who wants to be brave and go first?" No one said anything.

"I think what we need is a volunteer," Lima Bear said.

"Good idea," Whistle-Toe said. "I know. We'll all close our eyes and count to three. Everyone who wants to volunteer will raise a hand. Then when we open our eyes, we will see how many volunteers we have." So they closed their eyes and counted: one, two, three. No hands went up.

"Maybe someone did not understand the rules for volunteering," Lima Bear said. Whistle-Toe explained the rules again. Still, no hands went up. No matter what they tried, nobody volunteered.

"Hey, we have to be prepared," Whistle-Toe said. "What if the Cave Monster suddenly wakes up?"

"That's right," Maskamal said. "Back-Back, you stand near the cave and wave the flag. I'll stand over here with my bow and arrow." Maskamal moved far away from Black Cave - very far away.

"How are you going to hit him from there?"
Back-Back called out. "Your arrow won't go that far."

"It will if I pull back very hard. Besides, I can aim
better from a distance." Maskamal's knees were shaking.

There they waited and waited and waited.

"Hey Maskamal," Back-Back called out, "can I stop
waving this flag? My arm is tired."

"I guess so. My arms are tired too," Maskamal said.

"It will not be dark much longer," Whistle-Toe said.

"I'll go first," Lima Bear said suddenly.

So they lined up and started marching toward Black Cave: Lima Bear with the Royal Sword, Back-Back was next waving his flag, Whistle-Toe with his canteen, and then Maskamal far behind and crouching low. His hands were shaking so much that he could barely pull back on his trusty bow and arrow. They entered the cave. Everything became dark.

Act 3

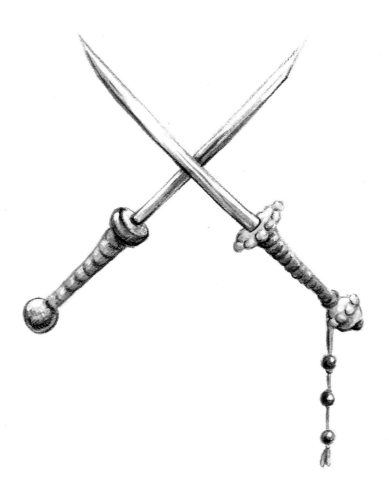

Deeper and deeper into Black Cave they went. It was dark except for the small fire the Cave Monster had lit to cook Sir L. Joe Bean in some bean soup. Every little noise they made seemed loud enough to wake a sleeping Cave Monster.

Lima Bear saw Sir L. Joe Bean tied up with spider-web rope. Quickly, Lima Bear cut him loose with the Royal Sword and handed it to him. Just then, they heard a roar and saw the Cave Monster. They were afraid. Back-Back waved his flag. But then he saw that the bow and arrow had dropped from Maskamal's hands. Whistle-Toe tried to hide behind his canteen. Sir L. Joe Bean held out the Royal Sword and Lima Bear picked up a tiny pebble to throw.

The Cave Monster first spotted Back-Back waving the red flag. He roared and Back-Back was so afraid that lay down to play dead, also making himself disappear. Now the Cave Monster saw only air.

Next, the Cave Monster saw Maskamal picking up his bow and arrow. The Cave Monster roared again and started toward him. Whistle-Toe threw his canteen at the Cave Monster to try to save Maskamal, but he missed. Sir L. Joe Bean and Lima Bear chased after the Cave Monster, Sir L. Joe Bean waving the Royal Sword and Lima Bear with his tiny pebble, but with their little legs they could not catch up.

Maskamal was so afraid that his eyes shut tight, and his hands pulled back on his bow so hard that it was pointing straight up. Then 'twang'. This time the arrow flew up…up…up, almost to the top of the cave, and then down…down…down. And it landed right on the Cave Monster's big toe. The Cave Monster cried out.

He jumped way up, up and down
And tumbled and rumbled round and round.
He jumped so high, he jumped so fast
That into the side of the cave he crashed.
And the big, big rocks up on the wall
Were shaken loose and they did fall.
They tumbled down and down and down
And buried the monster under the ground.
But the friends ran out, all safe and sound
And never again was the monster found.

"Maskamal, you're a great shot!" Lima Bear said.

"And so brave," Sir L. Joe Bean said. Whistle-Toe and Back-Back nodded.

"Yes, I was, wasn't I?" Maskamal said, proud of himself.

Sir L. Joe Bean was so thankful that he presented the Royal Sword to Maskamal. And that is how Maskamal came to be known as the best archer of the forest.